THIS FARM
is a MESS

written and illustrated by

LESLIE McGUIRE

PARENTS MAGAZINE PRESS / NEW YORK

A Parents Magazine
Read Aloud Original

Copyright © 1981 by Leslie McGuire
All rights reserved
Printed in the United States of America
10 9 8 7 6

Library of Congress Cataloging in Publication Data
McGuire, Leslie. This farm is a mess.
SUMMARY: Unable to stand the mess on Farmer Wood's
farm any longer, the animals decide to do something about it.
[1. Farm life — Fiction. 2. Domestic animals — Fiction.
3. Cleanliness — Fiction]   I. Title.
PZ7.M178Th   [E]   80-25811
ISBN 0 – 8193-1045-X
ISBN 0 – 8193-1046-8 (lib. bdg.)

To David...my constant
and unending source
of inspiration.

Farmer Wood had a nice little farm.
He had cows and pigs,
ducks and chickens, goats and sheep,
a mule, a dog and lots of cats.
He had all he needed for a good farm.

But things were not very good.
His farm was a mess!
Everything that wasn't worn or broken
needed painting or cleaning.
Each day things got worse.

Farmer Wood hadn't started the plowing.
The mule had eaten all the seed.
He said it was an accident.
"I thought it was my FEED," said the mule.
"This farm is a mess."

Farmer Wood headed for town
to buy more seed.
But the truck wouldn't start.
"I think I'll go lie down," he said.
"This farm is a mess."

No sooner had he settled
down for his nap than
all the cows clattered
into the living room.

"We haven't been milked
since yesterday,"
they mooed. "Besides,
we're staying here
until the barn is clean.
This farm is a mess."

Farmer Wood couldn't sleep.
He went to the kitchen
for a cup of coffee.

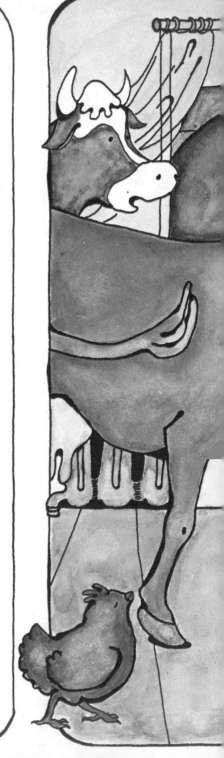

But he couldn't find a cup.
The cats had knocked over everything
looking for their cat food.

"Why worry about a few broken cups?"
meowed Herman the cat.
"This farm is a mess!"

Farmer Wood began to clean up
when he remembered he hadn't
collected the eggs.
The chickens were laying them
in the dining room because
Farmer Wood hadn't put a new roof
on the chicken coop.

Before he could collect the eggs, he saw the pigs in the garden eating the string beans and peas. "The corn is all gone," they oinked. "We were hungry."

STRING BEANS

Farmer Wood forgot about the pigs
and went to clean the yard.
"There is too much trash here,"
said Marvel the goat, "even for me.
This farm is a mess."

"Things cannot go on like this,"
Farmer Wood finally said to himself.
"I need a rest.
I'd like to win a trip — to anyplace.
For now I'll just lie down."

After his snooze,
Farmer Wood went
to fix a broken drainpipe
on the house.
All the animals were
sitting on the roof.
"We've talked it over,"
they said. "Things aren't
going too well here.
Why not take a trip to
the city?"

"I don't know,"
said Farmer Wood.
"What about the farm?"

"Don't worry,"
the animals said.
"We' ll take care of things.
Stay as long as you like."

So Farmer Wood set out for the city, and the animals got down to work.

The lambs did the laundry.

The cows took out the trash.

The animals mended the chicken coop, painted the tool shed, cleaned the barn, and fixed the truck.

But that's when they
ran into a problem.
No one knew how to plant things.

And no one could read directions.
"Anyway," said a pig,
"we have no money to buy seed."

In the morning the telephone rang.
It was Farmer Wood.
The animals tried to explain
their problem calmly.

"Help!" screeched a pig.
"Can you read?" asked the dog.
"Please come home," mooed a cow.
Farmer Wood said he'd be right home.

That afternoon, he came
puffing up the driveway.
He looked dusty and
rumpled, but he had
three bags of seed and a
part to fix the tractor.

"Say!" called Farmer Wood.
"Things look very nice."

"Oh, it was nothing,"
said the animals.
And they asked him
how his trip was.

"All right,"
sighed Farmer Wood.
"But I missed having
too much to do."

"We missed you too,"
said the animals.
"We can do a lot, but we
can't do everything."

"I know what you mean,"
said Farmer Wood.
"Being a farmer
is harder than it looks."

The dog asked, "If we
help you from now on,
do you think things
will be better?"

"I certainly do,"
said Farmer Wood.

So the animals carried
Farmer Wood's suitcase into the house.
The chickens helped him unpack.

The mule put the seed in the barn.
After fixing the tractor, they all
planted the fields.

Now, everything is the way it's
supposed to be on a good farm.
Each evening, Farmer Wood and
all the animals sit on the porch.
He tells them about the crazy things
that go on in the city.
Now that IS a mess!

ABOUT THE AUTHOR

LESLIE McGUIRE grew up on Long Island, right near the beach. When she was 12, her family moved to New York City. She has lived there ever since — now with her husband, and their young son. Ms. McGuire has taught art and special reading and has been a children's book editor. After her son was born, she turned to writing and illustrating.

Every summer, Ms. McGuire and her family visit her parents in the country, where there are a lot of farms. She says that she has never seen a messy farm there. She agrees with Farmer Wood that the city can sometimes be a mess — but despite that, she really loves it!